THE OGS INVENT THE WHEEL

Felicity Everett

Designed by Maria Wheatley
and Graham Round

Illustrated by Graham Round

Language and Reading Consultant: David Wray
(Education Department, University of Exeter, England)

Series Editor: Gaby Waters

First published in 1994 by Usborne Publishing Ltd, Usborne House, 83-85 Saffron Hill, London EC1N 8RT, England. Copyright © 1994 Usborne Publishing Ltd.

The Og family lived long ago in a place called Ogtown.

Pa

Ma

Grandpa

Zog

Mog

Grandma

One morning,
the Ogs were having breakfast
when Ned, the Ogtown postman,
called to deliver a postrock.

Everyone crowded around and Ma read the postrock.

ETHELBURGA
AND
EGBERT OG
!Invite you!
to the marriage
of their daughter Delilah
to Fustian Ponsonby-Thug
!———!
At The Fossil Town Cave
on Saturday.
2 o'clock sharp.

Where did Ethelburga and Egbert live?
(Clue: look at the back of the postrock).

6

So Pa got out some stone age snapshots.

The twins

Aunt Ethelburga

IGBERT

STIGBERT

Uncle Egbert

Delilah

What were the twins called?

7

And what about a wedding present?

What can you buy for the Ogs who have everything?

Grandma was already cooking something up. What do you think she was planning?

9

Grandma had decided to bake the wedding cake.

WEDDING CAKE

GRANDMA OG's RECIPE BOOK

I'll drop them a postrock to tell them it's all taken care of.

I'm sure they'll be thrilled!

Ma winked at Pa.

Grandma's cakes were famous in Ogtown - but not for their taste!

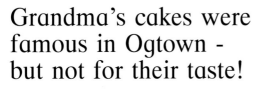

Zog's birthday cake had been ideal...

...as a doorstop.

The cake she baked for the Ogtown fair...

...had made the perfect birdbath.

Happy Anniversary

Can you see what Ma and Pa had used their anniversary cake for?

Saturday dawned,
sunny and bright.

The Ogs climbed on to Tiny,
their pet dinosaur, and
set off for Fossil Town.

Tiny was
usually
pretty zippy.

Come on, Tiny.
We're supposed
to be there in a
few minutes.

But Grandma's ten ton cake
made him slower... and s l o w e r .

13

...and ran slap bang into a woolly mammoth.

This was no ordinary mammoth. It was a Very Important Mammoth.

The Ogs could tell that by the way it was dressed up.

Who do you reckon is in there?

It must be some Fossil Town celebrity.

Who do you think might be inside?

Yes! It was none other than Delilah. And she was crying her eyes out.

How far does the wedding
party still have to travel?

17

The Ogs tried everything to get the mammoth moving.

They pushed.

They p u l l e d.

18

They offered bribes

and made threats.

I'll tell your Ma.

Nothing worked. Delilah was crying harder than ever.

Her bridesmaid wasn't helping either.

How many things is Delilah doing wrong?

19

and fell to the ground.

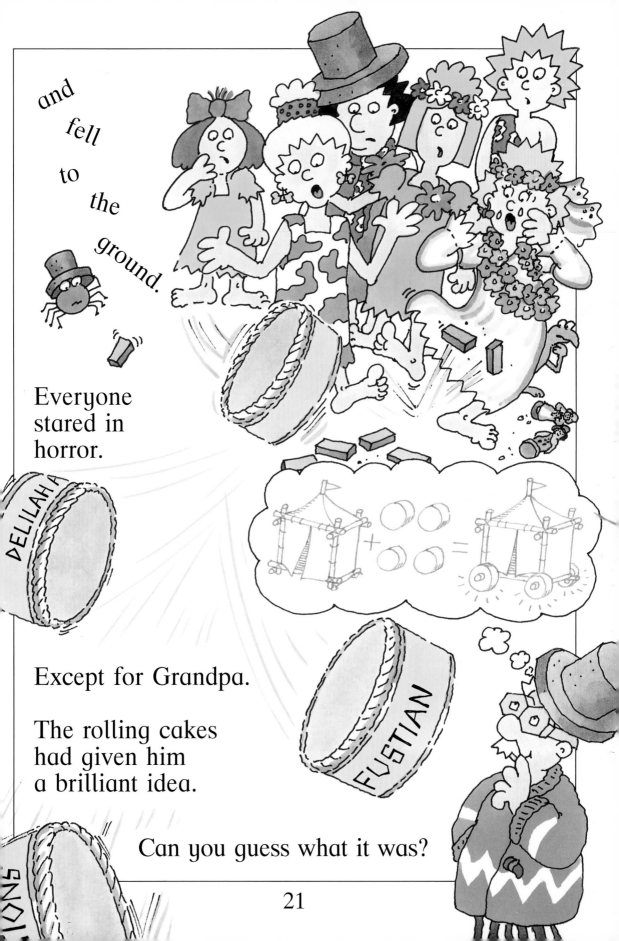

Everyone stared in horror.

Except for Grandpa.

The rolling cakes had given him a brilliant idea.

Can you guess what it was?

Thanks to Grandpa's idea,
Delilah got to her wedding
in the nick of time.

The other guests gasped
in amazement when they
saw her roll up.

23